Captured Up Close

20th Century Short-Short Stories

DC Diamondopolous

Author of *Stepping Up* (A Short Story Collection)

Cover Art and Story Illustrations: Wanda Baker
Cover and Interior Design: Rebecca Finkel, F + P Graphic Design, FPGD.com
eBook conversion: Rebecca Finkel, F + P Graphic Design, FPGD.com

Library of Congress Control Number: 2022908893
KDP softcover: 979-8-9862731-2-9
IS softcover: 979-8-9862731-0-5
eBook: 979-8-9862731-1-2

Fiction | Historical Fiction | Fiction Short Stories

First Edition
Printed in the USA

For Wanda

Acknowledgements

Thank you to the publications in which these stories first appeared.

1912: *Elipsis Zine*

1920: *Front Porch Review*
1920 was nominated by *The Winnow* in 2020
for Best of the Net Anthology

1929: *So it Goes: Kurt Vonnegut Museum and Library*

1932: *So it Goes: Kurt Vonnegut Museum and Library*
Semi-Finalist in the 2018 ScreenCraft Cinematic
Short Story Contest

1945: *Flora Fiction*

1946: *Down in the Dirt*

1951: *The World of Myth Magazine*
Member of the Month and Winner's Podcast
in 2018 from *The World of Myth Magazine*

1957: *Raven Chronicles*

1964: *Flash Fiction Magazine*

1968: *Sick Lit Magazine*

1970: *Progenitor*
1970 was nominated by *Progenitor* for the
2020 Pushcart Prize

1984: *Potato Soup Journal*

1992: *Progenitor*
1992 was nominated by *Progenitor* for the 2020
Pushcart Prize and was a Finalist in the 2021
ScreenCraft Cinematic Short Story Contest

With deep appreciation to: Wanda Baker, Cindy
Rankin, Pamela Hartmann, Vince DiCiccio, Barbara
Owen, and the Cambria Writer's Workshop.

Contents

Author's Note 1

1912: Invitation to Life 3

1920: Casting the First Ballot 11

1929: When All Seems Lost 19

1932: The Bonus Army 27

1945: Go Home and Make Babies 37

1946: First Time South 45

1951: Will Anyone Miss Them 55

1957: Life Before Stonewall 65

1964: The Beatles at the Hollywood Bowl . . . 73

1968: First Night Out 83

1970: Drafted 91

1984: All the Dying Young Men 99

1992: L.A. Riots 107

Acclaim for *Stepping Up* 116

About the Author 118

Author's Note

Flash fiction or short-shorts are stories told in no more than a thousand words. In researching the stories, I often traveled to the locations where they took place. My first short-short began with a story my mother told me that happened to her and my father in 1946 on a visit to the South. Each story in *Captured Up Close* was researched for historical accuracy. Except for the reference to historical figures, the characters in *Captured Up Close* are fictional.

1912

Invitation to Life

"Women and children first! Women and children first!"

A brandy snifter in one hand, a cigar in the other, I am alone as I watch people rush about on deck from the comfort of my leather chair in the first-class smoking room. It's past midnight, the lights flicker, but I am ruthlessly serene, for I did not overcome my childhood in the slums of the East End to drown in the freezing Atlantic water.

Second-class is where I belong, but who's to care now? When faced with death, we're all in the same boat.

Perhaps you've heard of me, Julian Grey, or seen my name on music hall marquees from Belfast to London.

I've made an enviable living as a comic, mimic, dancer, and acrobat. But what has brought me my greatest fame, and why I set sail on the Titanic to New York at the request of vaudeville manager, William Hammerstein, is my unfathomable ability to juggle five balls with my feet.

I put my cigar into an ashtray and set down the glass. Twisting the ends of my mustache, I am resolved about what I'm to do next, for I've never been one to pass up an opportunity.

I rise. The ship lurches. Poker chips, chess pieces, and tumblers fall on the floor. With my walking stick, I whack them away and stagger toward the door.

The ship creaks, a slow back and forth. The vessel tilts. I balance myself between the doorway.

The corridor is empty.

I open the door to a first-class suite. What finery, such elegance. There's a diamond stickpin and a ruby ring on the mahogany dresser. Did I mention that I am also a thief? I drop the stickpin and ruby ring into my coat pocket. I open the armoire and glide my hand over the dresses until I choose one.

If costumed in one lady's attire, I might draw attention, so I open the door to the next cabin.

"Excuse me, Sir," I say. A man holds a whiskey bottle in one hand and a Bible in the other. "Aren't you going on deck?"

"Leave me be young man."

I shut the door.

The next room is charming, even as the furniture slides to the wall, with peacock patterns on overturned chairs, an electric fireplace, a vanity fit for Sarah Bernhardt. Stumbling, I open a chest of drawers grab undergarments and a scarf.

What I need is a warm coat, ladies' boots, and a hat. The lights go off, then on. I must hurry.

I enter a suite across the hall.

The room is in shambles. The dresser is on its side, a chair on its back. I throw the clothes on the bed and go to the trunk and take out a winter coat, lace-up boots, and a hat with a feather.

What I am about to do may seem shameful.

I sit on the edge of the bed next to the heap of clothes and remove my coat, then my tie and collar. My brother, may he rest in peace, comes to mind as I unbutton my shirt.

The binding is tight around my chest, and I begin to unfasten. Charles, was more than a brother, a father, he was (I continue to unwind) to me, a motherless devil-rat, five years to his twelve. The bandage is off. My breasts are revealed.

I remove my trousers and drawers and pull the padding from between my legs. At a young age, Charles dressed me as a boy—"You'll be safer, and we can make a shilling or two." We performed on street corners and in taverns, and as I grew and girls liked me, I liked them back. I am not an impersonator like the popular music hall drags. I am a man, and I've made the best of my oddity.

Naked, I dress.

Perfumes from the clothes make my eyes water. I put my wallet, cuff links, and stolen jewelry into the pocket of the woolen coat and squeeze my feet into the boots.

There is a strangeness to it, and I feel an utter distaste, the way the undergarments rustle and swish. Above the dresser is a mirror. I put on the hat and cover my short hair but leave a fringe that falls over my forehead. The mustache, I peel off and put in my pocket.

Pinching my cheeks, the way I've seen my lovers do, I leave the way I came and go onto the deck.

Such chaos and panic. A man says good-bye to his wife and son as a lifeboat is lowered. Their cries provoke pity.

"Is there room?" I ask in a feminine voice.

"No, Miss," a crew member shouts. "Might be on the other side."

My unease mounts. I hurry among the crowd. My air of detachment collapses as I shove aside men and go around the stern. A lifeboat hangs from the davits.

"Women and children first!"

It's mayhem. Men implore their families to board, promising everything will be all right. From their shabby clothes, it's easy to see they're from steerage.

"What do we have here?" a shipmate yells. He removes a shawl and a scarf from the head of a man trying to board. "Josser."

A woman has the vapors and faints in her husband's arms.

A crowd gathers by a lifeboat hanging from the derricks. Men step aside as I make my way through.

Before me is a woman and her three daughters. Their tattered clothes arouse my sympathy. I slip the ruby ring into the woman's coat pocket.

"Come on, Miss," a deckhand says. He takes my arm and helps me into the boat.

Other than the two in command of rowing, I am the only man.

I dismiss any charge that I am a coward. Be that as it may, it will forever be a blessing, an irony indeed, that what saved me was the hand I was dealt.

1920
Casting the First Ballot

Aray of sun strikes the copper's badge and bounces off, lighting up the voting box inside H. L. Drugstore in me South Bronx neighborhood.

Now washed and mended, I wear the same once-blood-splattered and mud-stained dress, patched at the cuff, tattered 'round the collar. It shows the scars from when we marched down Broadway, I holding a sign, *The Vote For Equal Pay For Equal Work.*

It had started a glorious spring day, fresh from a night of rain, splendid with the radiance of blooming cherry blossoms. Little sister Annie pestered to come along. I told her, "Stay home with the youngins. You're too small and there might be trouble." She said, "I'm big enough and I'm a comin'. So there." And so she did, running along the sidewalk, keeping step with the march. Annie inherited the stubbornness that we McPhersons shared.

Hundreds marched. Me arms feeling the ache from holding the poster high above me head. Women clutched banners that stretched the avenue. Coppers on horseback, coppers on foot, looking for agitation—someone stirrin' the pot.

It did me heart good to protest among me own, knowing our numbers was a force to reckon with. Still an' all, we had to keep going, every day, every spare moment spent on the vote.

A man outside Woolworth's shouted, "Only vote I give you is a kick in the knickers."

Someone threw a rock. Glass shattered. Horses reared. Men broke through the lines.

Big oaf of a bloke grabbed me sign, slammed it hard on me head, he did. I fell to the ground.

"Lucy!" Annie's voice had the shock in it.

I sprawled in the street until I forced meself up. I looked 'round for me hat. I got to me feet and when I did something hit the back of me neck. I tumbled. Slumped on Broadway, staring at the buildings, the raging men, determined women, the world and all its unfairness swirling then dimmed.

Sirens, distant on the rim of me twilight, wailed, coming as a call to get meself up. On hands and knees, I was, when a copper kicked me in the chest. With great pain, I grabbed his ankle and raked short broken nails into his flesh. He shrieked. I rolled a ways over. Stood. For the sake of me sisters, I held up me fists like Jack Dempsey, but before I could sock 'em in the kisser two other coppers pulled at me shoulders, squeezed meaty hands 'round me breasts. I kicked. Sunk me teeth into their fingers. Their red Irish faces flushed with the memory of booze, their breath foul as the steerage our family sailed in across the sea.

They threw me into the paddy.

Father brought us here after mum died, for a new start, a better life. Working in a factory twelve hours a day, no windows, low pay, bosses forcing themselves on me. If I'd a had no father or brothers, I might a hated all men. But I and me family could eat. Back home, how can you march with an empty belly? So I wrapped hopes and dreams and those of me family in the red, white, and blue.

From inside the paddy, I looked over me shoulder for Annie. The riot swallowed her whole. *"Lucy!"* But I heard her voice shrill as a whistlin' tea kettle.

Across the aisle from where I was sittin' a woman with a gash on her cheek bled something fierce. I ripped off me cuff, dropped to me knees, and pressed it against the stunned woman's cheek. Through her tears, I saw eyes that kindled rebellion. The woman beside her began to sing, "Let Us All Speak Our Minds." The others, meself included, joined in the anthem. A copper in the front of the paddy banged his billy club on the grill and yelled, "Shut-up!" With no mind to the brute, we continued to sing. Louder. On the floor, a poster encouraged us with the words, *Never Give Up.* Our voices united, overpowered our fears, until he unlocked the gate and struck the nearest woman with his wooden stick.

Annie appeared, her thin arms waving as she ran alongside the wagon. I yelled through the bars, "Go home."

I, the eldest of six to me parents' brood, demanded a say in their raising and sending me brothers off to war.

Head aching, chest hurting, hair falling 'round me shoulders, me hat trampled somewhere in the fight. To jail I'd go. A criminal. A dangerous woman. I smiled at the notion and the girl who held me cuff to her head nodded as if reading me mind.

The wagon's siren split traffic with a blaring fright as we drove down Broadway and turned a corner. The Harlem River glimpsed between outdoor markets, shops, and eateries. Fear starting to get the best 'o me.

The jail full of suffragettes, there was no where to lock us up. So they let us go.

VOTES FOR WOMEN
BALLOT BOX

A year passed since the brawl as I waited to vote. I look into the faces of the women around me. Pride. A quiet jubilance. The change in our lives happening in this tiny drab storefront.

I think of the women who fought before us not having the chance to live this day. Do they know? I reckon they do.

I want to believe in something bigger now. That brotherhood will find the compassion to form a union for all of mankind.

I'm next.

A copper stands beside the ballot box, protecting the case with a scowl and a gun on his hip.

He motions me forward.

I keep me head high as I stride to the glass box. I write me vote in big letters and slip the paper into the slot as if planting something that one day will bloom.

I thank the good Lord for this day. Knowing that so shall life get better for me, it will get better for all.

When All Seems Lost

Douglas Haines was not an impulsive man. He'd given it a lot of thought—his decision final. He stood atop the Savings and Exchange Bank in the financial district of Los Angeles. The wide box toes of his oxfords suspended over the roof's ledge. Ten stories high, with no awning to catch a leg, the sidewalk empty, there would be no question of death.

He looked across Spring Street. The new city hall building dwarfed the Barker Brother's Furniture Company, Coulter Dry Goods, and every structure downtown. Giant candy canes and fake laurel were fastened to street lamps. Outside the post office a Santa Claus rang a bell over a donation pot, shouting, "Ho, ho, ho, Merry Christmas," mocking Douglas, who'd lost everything in the stock market crash.

Without money, how could he give to charity? There'd be no Christmas tree, no presents for his wife and daughter. Merriment had disappeared with his fortune.

He blamed the bankers, the stockbrokers, himself. Greed had grabbed him by the lapels. He remembered the seductive breath of it urging him to acquire more capital and with it the insatiable appetite for power. The country was drunk with wealth one moment, bankrupt the next.

If only he'd acted! The warnings of a crash had been threatening. First the September market crash in London. The papers promised the Rockefellers and Morgans would save them—*invest*. And there were his nightmares, for over a week, the same one. He was back in the war, in France, clawing his way through the mud to reach the Savings and Exchange Bank. With each handful of sludge, he slid further into an abyss. He'd wake up shaking, his nightshirt soaked. Mary would stroke his face. "It's just a dream, darling."

After the crash she reassured him that money didn't matter as long as they had each other and Lilly. How could she understand? She who was sheltered from the responsibilities of being a husband and father, supporting a family, protecting them, and if required, going off to war. What kind of man was he who had to send his wife and child to her parents' home in St. Louis—and borrow money for the train tickets from his father-in-law?

Now his gut acted up, repeated stabs that sometimes reached his chest. *Mary. Lilly. Hard to finish—thoughts, when . . .* he took a deep breath and found strength in taking charge of his death, a semblance of the person he'd been when supervising hundreds of men.

On the 8th floor below, he'd cleaned out his office— pictures of Mary and Lilly, pencils, pens, letters, awards, his pipe and tobacco, a photograph of himself smiling with the moving picture star Buddy Rogers at the ribbon-cutting ceremonies for Mulholland Highway. His life's work was packed in boxes, sealed against a future, neatly stacked, with all the edges touching, for Douglas Haines was a tidy man.

The Great War made him that way. His Springfield was cleaned, uniform buttons polished, everything in tip-top shape. Orderliness lived with him even as he stood on the mantel of the Savings and Exchange Bank: hair combed, shoes waxed, suit pressed.

In 1918, he'd wanted to desert—the bombs, grenades, pissing his pants from the fear of it. He endured but returned home, broken. Now as he gazed out at the dying bruise of a purple and yellow sunset, he *was* deserting. He had no money. A bum. Douglas was more afraid of living without honor, a name, a plaque on his office door announcing his achievements to all who entered, than stepping off a building.

He inched his shoes further over the ledge. Surely death would come in an instant. Then what? Not even the Carnegies or Vanderbilts knew the answer to that.

He saw derbies bobbing along the sidewalk. Where were the men going? Home? To other rooftops? That damn Santa ringing the bell. How come the sun sets—the moon rises? He looked up. There must be stars out by now in St. Louis. Had Lilly made a wish on the first one? He closed his eyes. Teetered.

He grasped his chest, leaned his upper body back. His left hand felt wrong. His thumb rubbed an empty space where his wedding ring had been—best ten years of his life. After he'd packed up his office, he left an envelope on his desk. Inside it he put his wedding band and wallet—also, a note to Mary telling her that he loved her and Lilly, and that he was sorry. Would she understand? And Lilly. A child needs a father. His body twitched. He was back in the war, felt the dank mire of the trench, shooting at the Hun, men dying, scared and homesick, longing to run away.

Steady, Haines, he told himself. Find courage in being, a—a what? A coward?

"Mary," he whispered.

He'd met her after the war. She brought everything that was good and clean and kind into his life, turning his dark world into one of wonder and hope. Then Lilly came. "Daddy's home!" Every night she'd run into his arms. It was the best tonic for a hard day's work. Who could love them more than he did?

He blinked, a hood of darkness flung over his future —never to see his child or hold the woman who brought him back to life. What would they think if they saw him standing on the edge of a building? How would his wife feel if she found him in the morgue? Could they ever forgive him for deserting them?

Douglas Haines was not a crying man. But tears for his family came hard, like a torrent. He took out his handkerchief and wiped his face. He stepped down from the ledge and crouched against the side of the building, shaking.

He stood, brushed off his suit, made certain his tie was centered and straight, then walked across the rooftop to the door and opened it.

1932

The Bonus Army

Pa decided to join the Bonus Expeditionary Force. After dropping Ma and the youngsters off at Uncle Vernon's, he let me ride the rails with him from our home in Waynesboro, Pennsylvania, all the way to the Washington Freight Yard.

Pa and thousands of other veterans were demanding their bonus pay—the money they could have earned if they hadn't gone off to fight for their country in the Great War. No man wanted to wait until 1945 to get paid, not while his family was starving. That's why we came to Anacostia Flats, a swampy, muddy area along the Anacostia River across from the Capitol where we could see the dome. Ankle-deep in mud, Pa and I built our shanty along with forty-three thousand, counting wives and children—the biggest Hooverville ever, named after the president who no one seemed to like.

When the bank people came to take our farm, Pa rushed out of the house with a shotgun and fired over their heads, scaring me and Joey. Ma cried. The twins howled and clung to her flour-sack dress. Pa cursed the politicians, said they were just bumping gums when it came to veterans' bonus pay.

We made our shack out of materials from the nearby dump site—old lumber, packing boxes, and scrap tin. Pa and I worked shoulder to shoulder. He started calling me Tom instead of Tommy.

Other veterans were scattered around Washington in deserted billets, but Camp Marks was the heartland. We built a real city with streets, latrines, a barber shop, a lending library where I spent most of my time, and a boxing ring, where Pa liked to spar.

For breakfast and dinner, everyone ate a stew made of potatoes, onions, and hotdogs. We lived on Pennsylvania Road, a place I called home.

Next door was a colored man from Harrisburg and his son Cornelius.

Pa said two things made a man equal—fighting for your country and taking care of your family—so it appeared, 'cause everyone got along. Pa said the newspapers lied, wanting to cause trouble, saying the races couldn't mix, and that communists were infiltrating the

WE WANT OUR
BONUS

camp. How could that be when everyone had to show their service certificate?

One day, Pa and I walked to the top of the bluff where we looked over the entire encampment. From poles and shanties, hundreds of American flags rippled in the breeze, showing how much we loved our country.

That night we took our meal back to our shack. Pa gulped his down and said, "War makes rich men richer. Remember that, son, before you go off to be a pawn in a rich man's game." I didn't eat much after that. Pa's anger and bitterness filled my belly instead.

A few days after we settled in, we walked to the Capitol where the House of Representatives took a vote on the Bonus Bill. Pa and I wore white shirts and bib overalls, wool caps—hot for June, but that's what we had, being farmers and all. Other men dressed in wrinkled suits and worn fedoras. The tall columns dwarfed the people on the steps. Veterans sang, "America," the air itself charged with hope.

When the organizer, Mr. Waters, came out and said the House passed the bill, I never heard such whooping and hollering. Tears ran down Pa's cheeks. Hats twirled in the air, cheering going on for near half an hour. We had money and could go home.

But when we headed back, Pa said, "Son, this is just one hurdle, the Senate has to pass the bill and that'll be harder."

"Why?"

"More Republicans in the Senate."

What seemed whacky to me was how something so sensible, like paying people their due, had to be voted on in the first place.

That night sleep came in jerks.

Two days after the House passed the bill, we went to the Capitol for the Senate vote. Veterans held signs reading, *No Pay We Stay, Give Us Our Bonus Or Give Us A Job.*

Pa's fists stretched the holes in the pockets of his overalls, his jaw working back and forth. I could feel him wanting to get into the ring while we waited. He took off his cap and looked to the heavens.

Pa's bonus money went down in the Senate. He said it was like the crash of '29 all over again.

I was too old to take his hand, but I let him take mine.

"We're staying on son, until justice is done."

Some folks left. But many stayed, with more coming from out west to join in the protest.

Toward the end of July, Hoover demanded that all veterans go home, but most had no home to go to.

On July 28, thousands of us walked to the Capitol. Food was becoming scarce at Camp Marks, so everyone looked gaunt, but we were righteous in our cause, and that gave us strength.

Police walloped the protesters with their billyclubs. We broke through their line and ran. Gun shots fired. Women screamed. It turned into a riot, and then I saw the U.S. Army marching toward us.

There was infantry, soldiers on horseback, tanks. They were coming to rescue us. Overjoyed, I cheered along with Pa and everyone else. The army aimed their rifles. Sunlight glinted off the tips of their bayonets. But then—

. . . they were charging at us!

Bile roared in my stomach. They hurled gas grenades. People scattered.

I hacked, snot poured from my nose. I experienced Pa's pain from being gassed in the war.

Veterans threw rocks at the army.

I shuddered, knowing my father could be killed by his own.

We ran toward the flats.

But what we were running to suddenly rose up in flames—the shanties, the library, all of Anacostia Flats.

Pa put his arm around my shoulder while we watched our city burn. I held back tears, wanting to be strong for my father.

1945

Go Home and Make Babies

I first saw Teresa out my kitchen window back in 1928. Her father, a widower, had moved into our neighborhood. I was kneading dough when I looked up and watched the child glide her sled down a snowbank and slam into a tree. I ran across the street. "Are you hurt?"

She scowled. "Mind your own beeswax."

I ignored her sass and asked if she would like a nice piece of hot homemade bread. She rubbed her bump with a snow-crusted mitten and shook her head. Teresa repeated the stunt and sailed free all the way to the sidewalk. I clapped my doughy hands. The little one smiled. "Can my pop have one too?"

The next year the stock market crashed, and we plunged into the Depression.

I'd see Teresa walk home from school, alone, shoulders slumped, eyes downcast. We all wore threadbare clothes, but her charity hand-me-downs never fit her growing body.

One day, I invited her to see Shirley Temple in *Bright Eyes*. Coming out of the theatre, she reached for my hand, such sweetness in her grasp. From then on I became her cheerleader, my pompoms the crocheted scarves and sweaters I made for her.

From the end of the Depression to another War, changes occurred every minute—and right here, in Farmingdale, New York.

In the winter of '42, Teresa got a job at the Brooklyn Navy Yard. I'd be at my window at six o'clock making dinner as she arrived home in a car full of girls. She ran with newfound joy up the steps to the front door, turned, and waved first to her friends then to me. Her smile brought riches not even Rockefeller could buy.

Teresa had every other Sunday off and we'd have lunch on my back porch. "Oh Aunt Lena, I never knew working with my hands could be so much fun. There's a lot of us gals, cutting and soldering, doing everything the men did. But our paychecks are nothing compared to what they earned."

"Of course not. Men have families to care for." My comment hung in the air like a barrage balloon.

Why, I never questioned my pay working in the factory during the First World War. It would've been unpatriotic—but this, I kept to myself. Now we could vote. Women smoked. Teresa wore overalls at work—so much had changed.

On a spring day in '43, she told me about her promotion. "I work on submarines, welding." She put down her fork.

"What's wrong, dear?"

"They're cramped quarters. My boss rubs up against me. When I told him to stop, he put me out in the rain to weld, knowing I'd get electrical shocks."

"Can't you go to his boss?"

She shook her head. "It's always the girls' fault."

I worried that after the war, young women like Teresa, who built our ships, tanks, and planes would question traditions. Men wouldn't stand for it. If I went to work, Roy would raise Cain, though he did let me sell war bonds.

In '44, Teresa made management, and our lovely Sunday lunchtimes came to an end. Her new boss, a decent man, depended on her. She worked twelve-hour days, seven days a week, and took care of her ailing father.

I helped out by sitting with Pop. One night when she returned late I expressed concern for her coming home alone in the dark.

She laughed. "With the boys gone, we girls can walk anywhere day or night and feel safe. Even Central Park."

Her breezy comment gave me chills. I saw thunder-clouds on the horizon. "You respect our boys who are fighting for our freedom, don't you?"

"Oh Aunt Lena." She put her arm around my shoulder. "Of course, I do. But women are fighting for freedom too. Just not on battlefields."

The war in Europe ended May 8, 1945, but it dragged on in the Pacific.

Teresa's final promotion came in early June. She over-saw seventy-five women in the construction department. I couldn't have been prouder of her.

On August 15, the radio blared, "Official! Truman announces Japanese surrender."

"Aunt Lena, Uncle Roy!"

We all had tears in our eyes as I opened the door.

"I'm going to Times Square, then on to the shipyard. Can you look in on Pop?"

"Of course, dear." A car waited for her. The girls waved flags. I held up two fingers making a V for Victory. "Do tell me everything that happens."

Roy and I went back to the radio. We heard about the thousands of people who turned out in cities across America. I imagined the red, white, and blue rippling and waving, confetti and ribbons, wet eyes and cheering —if only our beloved FDR had lived to see it.

That night we grew anxious as the hours passed and no word from Teresa.

The next morning I recall burning myself on the skillet. My mind filled with worry about our girl. Then from my kitchen window I saw her come out the front door. She wore slacks and a blouse and marched down the walkway to the car. Rigid—with dark smudges beneath her eyes.

I ran across the street. "What's the matter?"

"We wouldn't quit, so they fired us."

A girl in the car said, "With the boys coming home, we got canned."

"Of course. They'll need their jobs back."

Teresa glared at me. "My boss told me to get married and have babies."

"What did you expect?"

Teresa opened the car door. "I expected more from my country."

Back then I didn't understand the full impact of the war and what its aftermath meant to our daughters.

Now with Roy gone and Teresa out west, I think about those days and the car full of girls who worked at the Brooklyn Navy Yard. I know now as I watched them drive off to gather and speak up for their rights that what I saw was the future.

1946
First Time South

Snowflakes blew sideways down Main Street in Richmond, Virginia. It was Valentine's Day. Newlyweds, James and Betty Smith cuddled inside the trolley car. Betty took the cuff of her coat and brushed it across the window. Snow powdered brick buildings, running boards of parked Fords and Packards heaped with flurries, the sun paused low over the horizon. The Capitol was dusted in shades of gray.

They'd taken the train from their home in Philadelphia. It was their first trip south of the Mason-Dixon Line.

James had saved enough for a few days off and asked his bride where she would like to go. Ever since Betty saw *Gone With the Wind,* she wanted to visit the South.

Betty felt ritzy in her stylish beret, the mauve gloves and matching scarf arranged in neat folds around her neck. Cold air stung her bare legs. Though rationing ended it would be another year before she could buy nylons.

For their first day in the city, they went to the movies.

Back home, as she watched the coming attractions for *Gilda*, she just had to see the movie. When Rita Hayworth tossed back her luxuriant hair, her low-cut dress revealing a generous bust, and smiled at Glenn Ford, Betty dreamed of seducing James in just the same way.

She didn't have the sumptuous hair, or the opulent cleavage, and gosh dang it, she wasn't beautiful like all the good-looking dames in the movies, but she knew that James was dizzy in love with her.

The trolley clanged, stopped, and picked up a man in uniform.

Betty's nose touched the glass as she stared down the street and saw the theatre marquee with neon lights. There were so many people, bundled in wool coats and hats. They gathered in the portico, buying tickets at the box office. A column of people stretched beyond the roped off barricade, so many movie goers that another line began on the opposite side. Even on a cold late afternoon, half the city came out for the premiere.

"I'll get the tickets," James said.

Betty kissed his cheek. "I'll miss you, darling."

The trolley stopped. James tugged at the brim of his fedora. Betty hurried down the aisle and stepped into a cold gust of air.

She rushed to the shorter line, brushed snow from her coat, and tightened the scarf around her neck. People filed behind her, James waited at the ticket booth. He blew her a kiss. She beamed.

Betty heard grumbling. Of all the days to get into a snit, she thought.

Across the portico, an older man glared at her. Why, she wondered? She smiled back. Perhaps he had indigestion, or the biting wind triggered his rheumatism.

James put the tickets in his pocket and dashed to Betty. They nuzzled.

Low angry voices rumbled behind them.

Betty didn't move but glanced from side to side.

Two women in front looked over their shoulders. One scowled, the other clicked her tongue.

"Where's their southern hospitality?" Betty whispered to James.

"Beats me," he said and kissed her on the mouth.

Across the arcade, a woman shook her head and muttered.

Betty let go of her husband and stepped away.

"Hey, come here." James reached for her.

"No darling," she said, afraid she had offended their southern ladylike ways.

Muffled barbs. A woman cackled.

James took her hand.

"No darling. They don't like public displays of affection."

"Nuts!"

"They're genteel. I've heard that about the South."

A man across the way glowered and spat.

"Fuddy Duddy," James said, burrowing his fists into his coat pockets. "We're married." He yanked at his collar. "I spent four years fighting for my country, I have every right to hold hands with my wife."

Betty lowered her gaze and stepped further away from her husband.

She smelled aftershave lotion on someone behind her.

"Let's leave."

"You wanted to see this movie." James reached for her, wrapped his arms around her, and pulled her to his chest.

The crowd's pulse throbbed with a venomous beat, snaking its way around the colonnade.

"Please, James. Let's go."

People stepped out of line. Shoes squished. Twisted faces. Snarls. The mob moved in on James and Betty Smith.

Betty hung onto her husband's waist for fear they would tear them apart. Sweat soaked her blouse. She wanted to bolt. Run all the way back to Philadelphia.

"Trouble makers!"

"Wise guy!"

James' arms tensed. She felt his back muscles tighten. That frightened her more than anything. Open the doors, she prayed. She feared if they moved they'd be beaten to death.

"We've done nothing wrong," James shouted.

Atomic eyes. Incendiary mouths. Spurts of vapor.

The theatre doors swung open, two men ran out, and the older one yelled, "Break it up, move back!" He pushed through the crowd.

Someone shoved James.

He swung around. "Hey! Step out in the open and fight like a man. I'll bust your chops," he seethed.

Betty grabbed him and held on. "No darling."

"I said break it up!"

The younger man held out his arms, urging people to get in their lines. "Show's over. Except for the one inside."

The pack shifted, grunted, and slowly began to separate.

"You agitators or something?"

Betty glanced at his name tag, Manager Michael Buchanan.

"No," James said. "We were minding our own business. Just holding hands."

"All we wanted was to see the movie," Betty said.

"I'll handle it, darling."

"Where you from?"

"Philadelphia," James said.

"Can't you read?"

"Of course I can read."

"You're standing in the colored line."

Betty reeled. Her gloves hid her mouth. Her romantic image of the South was ruined forever.

"Northerners," he muttered. "Get in your own line and from now on remember where you are."

The young man stood at the door taking tickets from people across the portico.

Betty glanced around, ashamed, not for herself but for everyone there.

"Let's leave, James."

"You've been looking forward to this movie."

"Not anymore. Let's go."

1951

Will Anyone Miss Them

Charlie didn't have the guts to rob the drugstore in Visalia. The woman behind the counter reminded him of his mother—what a chump. His truck needed gas, oil, a new carburetor. No sweat. Now he could buy a brand-new Cadillac.

Charlie nodded at the man in the Air Force uniform. The goon thought himself important in his creased pants, pressed shirt, and two rows of medals on his chest. Charlie believed Roswell was a hoax, until now. Sure, he agreed. What crashed must have been a weather balloon.

"Take anything?" the goon asked.

"Nope."

"Touch anything?"

"Nope."

"How long you been here?"

Charlie shrugged. "A couple minutes," he said, glancing at his truck.

"Your truck?"

"Yeah. Can I go?"

"In a few minutes. Stay here." The goon walked off.

Charlie had been driving to the Paradise Motel when he saw an oblong craft zigzag across the sky. It cartwheeled over the flatlands of Bakersfield, then bam, a boom so loud the wheels on his truck wobbled. He parked. Ran to the crash. Fear smacked him to his knees. A huge gash in the ship exposed four bodies. They had webbed hands and their skin was scaly, like a snake. Two were embedded in the control panel, the other two twisted in the wreckage. They oozed an orange slime and reeked of rotten hamburger. Charlie pitched forward. Vomit gushed from his mouth. He wiped his face. Stood. Shaking. Walked backwards—staring. Halfway to his truck, it registered, he'd hit the jackpot!

He jammed his pockets with debris strewn across the field—trophies from the crash—elastic metals, a tube with symbols, a dial with knobs around it. The largest piece was a weightless inlaid screen. He could live on the story for months, maybe years—no more jail time. Gladys would take him back. Charlie was gonna be rich.

He had gone to his truck, wrapped his loot in rags, and crammed them under the seat next to his gun. He started over again until he heard sirens. In the distance, he saw flashing lights, heard helicopters overhead. Too far from his truck to split, he dropped the goods and ran.

The military goons suited up in white jumpsuits, masks, and gloves. Oh, shit, contamination. He hadn't thought of that. He looked at his hands, his bare arms, ran his fingers over his stubble—nah, nothing to worry about.

The cops arrived and then the press with their cameras. The military ordered everyone off the land. Charlie liked seeing the cops get the shaft for a change.

Leaning against the fence post, he pulled a match and a cigarette butt out of the sleeve of his rolled-up T-shirt. He gazed at the crash site. Man, where the hell did they come from? It was no flying saucer, and no little men with giant heads. These things were like reptiles. Did they have families? Would anyone miss them? Charlie blew smoke into the dry summer air. Damn. He was starting to feel sorry for them.

The whole crazy scene made him look to the skies. It made him think. He tried to grasp something, but it was beyond his understanding—beyond where to get his next lay or his next buck. The wonder of it all made him curious and scared all tangled into something bigger than himself.

The same goon walked toward him. "Come here, Bud."

The guy put his arm around him. Charlie tried to shrug him off, but the goon stuck his claw into his shoulder.

They walked parallel to the site, the man's hand clamped around him.

"Turned out to be a gag. Kid's prank," the goon said. "We don't want rumors. You know. Scare people—have everyone panic." He released Charlie. "You understand?"

"Sure I do."

The guy handed him three twenties.

Charlie hadn't seen that much dough since he knocked off a hardware store in Fresno a year ago. He grabbed the hush money and stuffed it in his pocket.

"You can go."

Charlie headed toward his truck. He saw a convoy of jeeps and vans on the highway coming toward them. A lot of fuss for a joke. The big shots thought they could bribe him.

He opened the door and climbed into the Chevy. Charlie stuck his hand under the seat and felt for the stash. It was there. So was the gun. He switched on the ignition. It wouldn't turn over. He tried it again—and again.

"Something wrong?" the goon asked.

"My truck's dead. You got cables?"

"No. Where's the nearest filling station?"

"A few miles west of here," Charlie said, feeling the jitters.

"Any diners around?"

"Yeah."

"My driver will take us."

Damn truck was always breaking down. With the sixty bucks he could have it towed and fixed, then sell the heap of junk.

A jeep crawled up beside him.

"Get in. I don't have all day," the goon said from the back seat of the car.

Charlie locked his truck and climbed into the jeep.

"Got a cigarette?" he asked the driver.

"Yeah."

Charlie cupped his trembling fingers around the flame. He stared at the crash site. What will they do with them? Images of those poor bastards would live with him till he died. He shot one last glance at his truck with the goldmine inside.

"Don't worry about your truck," the goon said. "It's not going anywhere."

"Who said I was worried." He stubbed his cigarette and tossed it out the window.

The stretch of land was one long road out in nowheresville. Purple sage, sycamore trees, tumbleweeds, the mountains in the distance—if he could live anywhere he'd still choose the San Joaquin Valley. He heard rustling behind him. Then the barrel of a gun pressed into—what did Gladys call it, his sweet spot. They were gonna kill him all along.

Charlie took a deep breath and looked at the wide-open skies and wondered if anyone would miss him.

1957

Life Before Stonewall

Welcome to The Shady Lady, a queer bar in San Pedro, California, across the railroad tracks, near the docks, in a back alley off Harbor Street. It's a raunchy hole in the wall dive where dykes and drag queens hang. So you didn't think they mixed? Well, think again Daddy-O. Over there, slouched against the juke box, listening to Gogi Grant croon "The Wayward Wind," is Stormy, a big broad-shouldered butch who flirts with anyone who has tits and a pussy. Cigarette clamped to the side of her pouty James-Dean-like lips, she can talk, play pool, and switch-blade her way out of a fight, and the L&M never moves a lick. Her hair is greased with pomade and combed up on the sides with a pompadour rising like a tidal wave from her forehead. On the outside Stormy appears cool, but on the inside her stomach is doing wheelies. You see, a bust is about to happen, and she knows it.

Stormy yanks the jukebox plug from the wall. "It's the fuzz!" she shouts.

The teeny-weeny dance floor empties. The pool table is abandoned. Everyone scatters to small wooden tables and bar stools.

Stormy struts to the center of the room. "If the man rounds us up, fight back, you dig?"

"No sweat," someone answers.

Across the room, under the exit sign, meet VaVoom, a six-foot-five drag queen in stiletto heels raising her height to a near sky-scraping altitude. She wears a floral skirt with mesh petticoats, a black low-cut blouse, and a choker of fake pearls just below her Adams apple. Her short, Italian-styled wig is from Max Factor of Hollywood, and her layers of false eyelashes from Ohrbach's. She holds a cue stick like a ball bat. No way is VaVoom going to let Johnny Law give her the royal shaft.

Blue and maroon vice cars surround the seedy bar. Parked outside the lonely hideaway, the Black Mariah waits to haul off the sickos.

A gust of fish and gasoline swooshes in through the entrance. It's another night in the city where the heat gets their kicks hassling stompers, fems, and swishes.

"Okay motherfuckers, let's go. The freak show's over and the paddy's outside," a cop shouts.

"Didn't you get your pay-off?" a queen with a falsetto voice asks.

"Shut-up."

VaVoom hits the breakers.

Blackout!

Crash! Boom! Bam! Pop!

The Shady Lady turns into a blind noise of sticks swooshing, pool balls cracking, and feet scuffling. A flashlight cuts across the ceiling like a search-light at a movie premiere, but this ain't no movie. This is where dreams turn to pulp.

A fist slams Stormy in the back. "Ohh," she moans.

A stick strikes a skull.

A scream freeze-frames the moment.

It's our heroine VaVoom, holding the bloody cue. She shoves open the back door, swings the pole across the face of the cop guarding the exit and knocks him to the ground.

"Ahh," he cries and covers his broken nose.

VaVoom grabs Stormy. "Follow me."

"Where to?" Stormy asks.

"Hush-hush," Vavoom says. "It's very confidential." She pulls off her heels and sprints down the back street like Elroy "Crazylegs" Hirsch.

Stormy grips her cigarette between thumb and fore-finger and flicks it away. She bolts after VaVoom.

EXIT
THE
SHADY LADY

Under a full moon, they run past cargo crates and pallets. The stink of diesel and garbage hangs in the air. The two escapees turn the corner at a cannery and dart alongside the Port of Los Angeles. Lights from Terminal Island flicker across the harbor. To the south, oil derricks and wells pump in an urban field of dinosaur spiders in 3-D. They both know what happens if caught—booked, fingerprinted, their names listed in the Daily Breeze under perverts. Lives ruined.

Stormy catches up to the towering drag queen. "Where the hell are we going?"

"To my boat," she says in a high-pitched breathy pant. "It's fabulous."

"You have a boat?"

"I dock in Long Beach," the transvestite says, gulping air. Her wig slips. She tugs it forward with one hand while dangling the straps of her heels with the other. "And sail here." She hurries toward the wharf.

Stormy charges after.

VaVoom runs down the pier to a small wooden cabin cruiser and unties the rope. She lifts her skirt and long legs over the edge and steps into the boat. It rocks. Water ripples and gurgles. She opens the door to the cabin and disappears inside.

Stormy climbs into the boat. The cruiser laps from side to side. The door creaks back and forth.

"C'mon. Let's split." VaVoom's voice dips an octave. She fires up the engine.

Stormy swings open the door and steps inside. The crossdresser sits at the helm with her back to her. The queen's wig and stilettos are on the table. She runs a large hand over her crewcut, then peels off the blanket of eyelashes.

The big butch sits beside her partner in crime and lights a cigarette.

VaVoom powers the craft away from the dock and heads toward Long Beach.

"Thanks," Stormy says around the filter of her L&M.

VaVoom wipes her lipstick off with a tissue. She turns.

Stormy's cigarette falls to her lap. "Mr. Hazzelrigg!" she says, staring into the face of her tenth grade math teacher.

"It's good to see you again, Mary Louise."

1964

The Beatles at the Hollywood Bowl

When Dawn saw the Beatles on Ed Sullivan she understood what those women in her mother's dirty books were talking about. Her life changed from sunshine and lollipops to a screaming fit of juvenile ecstasy more powerful than an atomic bomb. Bye, bye, Frankie and Annette. Hello John, Paul, George, and Ringo.

Dawn squealed from the front seat of her father's black Cadillac de Ville. She glanced back at her best friend, Judy. "Look," she said, feeling her braces scrape the inside of her cheeks. She winced and pointed to the Hollywood Bowl's marquee. *Tonight 8:00 P.M. "The Beatles In Concert" Sold Out.* "I think I'm going to faint." She lifted the Brownie to her eye and clicked the camera's button.

Hundreds of kids rushed along Highland Avenue. Police guided traffic, waving their arms, blowing whistles.

"My God," Dr. Murphy said. "You'd think it was V-Day."

He drove his car into the side entrance and rolled down the window. "My wife's on the board," he said to the security guard, pointing to the sticker on the windshield. "I'm dropping off my daughter. I've never seen anything like this. Kids all the way down to Hollywood Boulevard."

"They camped out overnight," the guard said, shaking his head. "It's crazy."

"Dawn, don't do anything to embarrass your mother."

"I'm not a baby."

"Hang on to that camera. I'll pick you up at 10:00."

"Thank you, Dad. You're the best."

"Thank you, Dr. Murphy," Judy said.

Dawn and Judy walked down the incline, the strap of the Brownie gripped tightly in Dawn's hand, photography as much a mania for her as the Beatles.

Girls dashed out from the underground tunnel. They jammed the footpath, bodies spilling over inside the moving walkway—a stampede of teenagers with zits, headbands, and Aqua Net flips. Their mothers' Jean Nate perfume whiffed through the frenzy.

A yellow haze circled the warm August evening below a pale blue Los Angeles sky.

"Everyone's gone ape," Dawn said. "Including me," she shrieked, grabbing the sides of her head. "Let's go, Judy."

Dawn squeezed her chubby body through the crowd, dragging her friend behind.

At the gate, she reached into the pocket of her lavender peddle-pushers, pulled out two green tickets, and handed one to Judy.

"I know where to sit," Dawn said to the attendant. "I come all the time."

Dawn hurried through the gate. Reserved Section Row J 17 38. "Eee, look at our seats," she cried, sweeping her blonde bangs out of her blue eyes.

"Box seats. Second row. Center," Judy said, clutching her heart. "I am *so* stoked."

Inside the box were four seats. Dawn and Judy took the front two. Dawn turned and snapped a picture of the rising tiers as thousands of girls crammed the aisles. She took photographs of people in trees and the surrounding Hollywood Hills.

Giddy, she aimed the Brownie at the stage with the pool in front. She took a picture of Ringo's drums sitting high on a platform.

The sun ducked behind the canyon as teenagers reached their seats. The lights in the Bowl turned on.

Dawn wriggled her shoulders and moved her bra straps—something new since she'd grown boobs as big as her mothers. She straightened the pink bow above her bangs, made sure the clip was tight and centered—just in case Paul looked at her. Because of her braces, she refused to smile when Judy took her picture.

At 8:00, a man walked on stage. When he said the word *Beatles,* Dawn and over 18,000 girls screamed a mating call to their heroes.

The host introduced Jackie deShannon. She sang her hits. The Righteous Brothers followed. Dawn clapped politely, drummed her foot, propped her flip with the palms of her hands, and waited for the fab four from Liverpool, England.

When the last act left the stage, a hush spread around the amphitheater.

The host came out and presented the KRLA deejays. In unison they said, "And now here they are, *The Beatles.*"

Dawn and everyone erupted into screams. The noise so great Dawn couldn't hear herself.

Girls stood in the aisles. Camera bulbs flashed. The Hollywood Hills twinkled with lights.

Tears rolled down Dawn's baby-fat cheeks. She raised the Brownie, but with the emotion of seeing her idols up close—the sexy way John sang, "Twist and Shout" with his legs slightly spread and, oh, Paul, so dreamy—Dawn stopped snapping pictures and just let herself bawl.

THE BEATLES
KODAK
BROWNIE CAMERA
HOLLYWOOD BOWL
Symphonies under the Stars
TONIGHT - 8:00 P.M.
THE BEATLES
IN CONCERT
SOLD OUT

She peeked at Judy pulling her hair, wailing.

If Dawn wanted to be another Margaret Bourke-White, she thought, she'd better get with it. She wiped her eyes, lifted the camera, and aimed it at Paul. But the girls in the first row kept jumping up down, waving their arms, and the clutz next to her was jabbing her elbow into the side of Dawn's head.

Dawn pushed past the bozo and grabbed the edge of the box-seat. Girls ploughed into each other. Dawn forced her way down the steps until she stood behind the pool.

She lifted the Brownie. Bad angle. Standing on tiptoes, she held the camera above her head. Someone shoved her, and the Brownie went flying over the pool. Dawn lunged, caught it in midair, bellyflopped into the water with her arms extended, saving her camera from ruin. "Ohh," she yelped. Drenched. Her teeth chattered, face hot. But what a vantage point.

Dawn waded to the ledge, put her elbows on the platform, and clicked pictures a pro would be proud of. She saw a cameraman in the wings with a press pass pinned to his shirt taking pictures of *her*. Oh no, if her mother found out she'd ground her for a year.

Fans leaped into the pool, splashing and slopping water, trying to heave themselves onto the stage.

Guards arrived and fished the girls out.

Dawn looked up at Paul. He winked at her and grinned, a smile that gave her heart wings.

1968

First Night Out

Johnny kneeled on top of his bookcase as he wiggled the screen out of its frame and let it slide onto the bush outside his bedroom window. Just as he raised his leg over the ledge, he remembered his retainer and yanked it out of his mouth, tossed it onto the dresser, and climbed out.

Sneaking around the side of the house, he unlatched the gate, inched through, then locked it. He glanced west toward the Brewers' house and east to the Fillmores'. At ten thirty at night, the neighborhood had tucked itself into bed. His old man's station wagon parked in the driveway was a real daddy's car, but it had wheels, and that's what Johnny needed to take him to his first gay bar.

Johnny pulled his dad's key from his crushed velvet pant pocket, unlocked the car, and slipped behind the wheel, leaving the door ajar. He put the gear in neutral and let the Buick roll back into the street and then pushed the car past the Wilsons' house, shut the door, started the engine, and took off for the Harbor Freeway and Santa Monica Boulevard.

When he had read in the local paper that his science teacher was arrested in a raid at The Rusty Nail and lost his job because he was a homosexual, Johnny felt bad for Mr. Gilroy, but excited to know he wasn't the only queer in the universe. The Rusty Nail reopened as a bar for men and women, *gay* men and women, Johnny learned through the back pages of the underground press.

Johnny pounded his fist against the wheel, feeling the victory of freedom. He had the fake ID his sister's boyfriend made for him, thinking Johnny wanted to meet some fox at the Blue Turtle, but with a constellation of zits on his chin, his voice still swinging between the Little and Big Dipper, Johnny's chances of making it through the doors of The Rusty Nail were still slim.

Three days before he got his driver's license, Johnny rehearsed punching and fluffing his pillows like he'd seen prison escapees do in the movies, then he pulled the cover over them to make it look like a body underneath. He practiced climbing out the window so he wouldn't mess his clothes by falling into the bush that grew outside his bedroom. He committed the perfect getaway until he realized he'd left the Free Press with the big red circle around The Rusty Nail lying on his desk. No sweat. He'd be back before his parents woke-up.

Johnny rolled down the window just enough so that it didn't disturb his long hair that he brushed and groomed until his arm felt tired. When he had missed several hair cuts, his father told him he didn't want his son looking like a queer. Johnny told his dad not to worry, he hated fags, but long hair was in.

His dark mop covered his ears, and he grew really cool sideburns.

If his old man saw him now in his bitchin' yellow striped and red polka-dot shirt and Nehru jacket, driving his car, he would flip.

Johnny drove up the onramp. Too bad he wasn't in a boss looking Mustang instead of an old fogey's car. He'd park a block away from the bar so no one would see it, but what if he met someone? It was his uncle's car, he'd tell them, because his Mustang was in the shop. Lies. That's what his life was about, dating girls, football, acting tough, all to please his dad and everyone else. He even put up a poster of Raquel Welch when he wanted to tack up Steve McQueen.

RUSTY
NAIL
BUICK

Johnny's secret gave him headaches. It was a monster that gobbled him up until he felt like he'd become the thing that consumed him. Something dirty. Something that made guys pick fights with him. He hoped to replace loneliness with friendships and meet a cute guy at the bar.

He relaxed into the flow of the cars, turned on the radio and switched the dial to KRLA and Dave Hull, the Hullabalooer.

"Mony Mony" blasted through the speakers. Johnny thought he would explode with pleasure. The sexy beat sparked his fantasies into a rocket fueled ascension where dancing led to kissing and kissing led to hot sex and hot sex never ended.

His loud singing drowned out Tommy James. He took his hands off the steering wheel and clapped along with the Shondells laughing and hollering, "Yeah, yeah, yeah, yeah!"

Johnny zoomed past downtown and veered into the lane for the Hollywood Freeway. He slouched down in the seat, his left hand hanging over the wheel, real cool, like he'd done it millions of times. He glanced left, then right, just to see if anyone was lucky enough to see how groovy he looked.

He reached in the glove compartment and took out his dad's cigarettes. Shaking one free, he stuck it between his lips then punched in the lighter. It popped out, and he lit the cigarette. He took a drag and coughed. His eyes watered. He puffed without inhaling.

Someone pulled in front of him.

"Asshole!"

Johnny stepped on the gas and swerved into the fast lane.

"Wanna drag? I can make this mother move."

He stubbed out the cigarette and caught up with the guy who almost creamed him. The jerk wasn't even paying attention to him, probably didn't even know he almost caused an accident. Johnny blared the horn. The guy gave him the finger. Johnny laughed. He had to be at least eighty, older than his grandparents.

He passed the Melrose exit. The Western offramp would be next, and he'd take it to Santa Monica Boulevard.

He flattened the gas pedal all the way to the floor. Street lamps flickered by, he felt the air lift his hair, smelled the damp night and asphalt. Johnny glanced in the rear-view mirror. Red lights flashed. A siren screamed.

1970

Drafted

Drunk and stoned, Scott staggered out the door of the Whisky a Go Go and into the night. A blurred neon sign from the Sunset Strip flickered and shuddered through the ebb-and-flow haze that hovered from his high. The notice to appear before the local draft board was crumpled deep in the pocket of his bellbottoms like a wet snot rag.

He lit a Camel. "Happy birthday to me, but who gives a shit," he shouted at a group of foxes in hot pants. "I'm gonna go to Canada, wanna come?"

Jelly brained, Scott closed his eyes and leaned his bushy blond head against the building until his knees buckled, and he landed on his ass. He blew a stream of smoke up at a three-story-high billboard of Linda Ronstadt, then flicked the cigarette across the pavement.

"Fuck-off. Go on. Get outta here," said the bouncer, standing outside the entrance to the club.

Scott crawled to his knees as a wave of barf started to peak. He ran up the sidewalk to the back of the Whisky and threw up on the steps of the fire escape. With the bottom of his tie-dyed T-shirt, he wiped his mouth, felt better, took out another smoke, and lit it.

He didn't have rich parents who could get him out of the war, he wasn't a psycho, and no way was he queer. He didn't have the grades or want to go to college. His passions in life were drawing and surfing. The only thing left was to run away to Canada. But Scott hated the cold, and there were no decent beaches. When his father saw him sketching, he'd say, "You'll never make a living at that sissy artsy-fartsy stuff. Cut your damn hair. Join the military. Be a man."

If he did go to Nam, he'd kill people he had no beef with. When he told his old man this, he exploded, "Communism must be stopped. Or we'll all be talking Russian." His mom stood in the background nodding and silently crying.

When the National Guard killed four students at Kent State, his father told him they deserved to be shot for protesting the war. Scott was dumbfounded. "What about My Lai? Did innocent Vietnamese deserve to be raped and murdered by U.S. soldiers?" "That's war," his dad snapped. "It happened in WWII. Korea. It's no surprise it happened again." His dad's answer blew his mind.

Scott asked him if he'd been born German would he have sent Jews to the ovens. His father said, "I would have followed orders, that's what soldiers do." "Then you'd be a murderer," Scott yelled. His dad slapped him. Shocked, Scott held back his rage from wanting to wallop his old man and beat the callousness out of him, but that smack turned the shine on his father's pedestal to rust.

It was hell living with his family in Hawthorne. Scott moved out, got an apartment, a job at Mattel. He hated the nine-to-five monotony of assembling Barbie Dolls for a paycheck and the tired empty feeling of coming home, getting drunk, smoking pot. He missed the old days when he and his dad fished off the Redondo Beach Pier. He missed having a father.

Simon and Garfunkel's "Bridge Over Troubled Water" boomed then faded from a car as it cruised the Strip.

His childhood friend, Robbie, had come home in a body bag. For what? Their generation was screwed. He had no say about the war because he couldn't even vote. If attacked, Scott would gladly take a bullet for his country. But this war? He slid down the wall of the Whiskey, dragging his angst with him.

His mother called that morning, wishing him a happy birthday. She told him his father loved him. Then why didn't he call? Scott knew why. His father was stuck in a time warp when going to war was heroic. His dad thought him a coward for not wanting to fight. His parents would freak if he'd run away to Canada.

He stubbed out the Camel and brushed vomit off his sandals.

Through the mist of his high, a mellow warmth broke through. He took out the crumpled draft notice, smoothed and folded it, and stuck it in his pocket.

He needed to draw. He imagined his hand flying across the page, creating a world of his own. It calmed him, made him feel in control. Not even sex could do that.

Scott turned away from the glitz of Sunset, the shimmering lights of the city beyond, and headed up Clark.

His mom's '58 Ford Fairlane—last year's 18th birthday present—with the remaining scraps from the peeled off bumper sticker, *America Love It Or Leave It,* was parked up the hill.

A group of hippies walked toward him.

"Peace man," one of the guys said, holding up the V sign of his right hand as he passed.

"Yeah, man. Peace," Scott said without hope, his strong young body to be used as a killing machine.

He unlocked the Ford, took out his drawing pad and pencil, and sat on a low concrete wall facing Sunset and downtown L.A.

DRAFT CARD BURNIN HERE
AMERICA
LOVE IT OR LEAVE IT

Street lanterns and outdoor apartment building lights cast ominous shadows from manzanita plants.

Scott could have drawn in total darkness, so clear was the picture in his mind, the certainty of his decision.

With the pad on his knees, he sketched the sun setting on a beach in South East Asia with a sandy coastline, palm trees, bamboo boats.

He heard the rat-a-tat-tat of machine guns in the jungle, hissing insects, the smell of death in the rice paddies.

The sprinklers came on and he jumped up, shielding his paper. But Scott liked the river of tears running down his drawing, leaving their trace on his dying body as he took his last breath on the shore of the South China Sea.

All the Dying Young Men

James, as the doctors and staff at St. Mark's Regional Hospital in San Diego insisted on calling him, applied pancake make-up over the band-aid camouflaging the skin lesion on his chin. He was glad to be home, surrounded by his Nippon figurines, the ornate lampshades with exotic scarves draped over the top, and his trunk of overflowing satin and silk costumes, boas, several strands of pearls, and oodles of costume jewelry. His move to San Diego had been a windfall—the most money he'd ever made doing drag. He lived to entertain. On stage, he was Jasmine and loved. Standing-room only. Now he was sick. How long would he be able to afford his apartment in Hillcrest?

The obituaries from three newspapers spread across the coffee table. Circled in black were the names of seven young men.

Jasmine wanted to live, to work again at Glitter Glam Drag. But James didn't.

No can do, James. You're not going to pull me down today. It's Pride. I'm going to party.

Donna was coming.

At St. Mark's, the only person who bathed and dressed him, changed his sheets and consoled him, was Donna, the pretty dyke nurse who was now his source for food, medication, and shots—his entire life.

It was Sunday, her day off, and she promised to take him to Pride. Jasmine had never missed a parade, but James's taunts of looking butt-ugly opened more scabs than he had on his body.

Jasmine dressed in black sweatpants and a gold lámay blouse, brushed her long stringy hair, pulled it into a ponytail, and clipped it with a rhinestone barrette. She applied red lip gloss and blue eyeshadow.

When James fell ill and admitted himself to St. Mark's Regional, the doctor asked how many men he had slept with. *Was he kidding?* "Honey, how many stars are there in the heavens?" Hundreds, thousands, in parks, bath houses, clubs, from San Fransisco to LA and San Diego. The doctor had kept a straight face when James answered. The nurse turned her back on him.

Gay liberation tore the hinges off closet doors. Men like him left the Midwest for the coasts and found a bacchanal of men, a confectionery of sex and drugs, a

feast for the starving who thought they were alone in the world.

James's life had been about dick and where to get the next fuck. Jasmine's life was drag, antique stores, and *Vogue Magazine.*

When his conservative, homophobic, fundamental Christian parents caught him in his mother's dress and high heels, they demanded, "Get out now and don't you ever come back." He promised them, "I'll live up to your expectations. I'll make the most of a trashy life."

Jasmine grabbed a green boa from the trunk and wrapped it around her neck. *You think that'll hide your Kaposi's Sarcoma,* James baited. Jasmine tugged at the feathers that made her neck feel on fire.

Grace Jones's, "Pull up to the Bumper" boomed from the ghetto blaster. Jasmine wanted to dance, but her legs ached. *You can't even walk, sucker.*

"Shut-up, James." Jasmine said, pulling herself up and moving to the window.

When he heard a car, he backed out of view. James never wanted Donna to know what she meant to Jasmine.

He held onto furniture as he made his way to the red velvet couch and sat, poised, waiting.

Donna knocked and opened the door.

"Well, don't you look jazzy," she said, pushing a wheelchair inside with a rainbow flag attached.

You'll look like a sick bastard in that baby buggy,
James bullied. Everyone will know you have AIDS.

"I can't go."

"It's up to you."

"Are we so pathetic we need a parade?"

"Yes." Donna pinned a button that read, *Gay by birth,*
fabulous by choice, on his blouse. "We need to pump
ourselves up. If we don't, who will?"

"They want all queers dead. Looks like they'll get
their way."

"Not everyone. The Blood Sisters keep donating
blood, and they're delivering food and medicine."

"Thank God for lesbians," he said and wondered if
gay men would do the same if lesbians were dying.

Donna released the footrests on the wheelchair.

"I'm not going. Everyone will know I have AIDS."

"You do, James."

He looked away, not wanting to disappoint the woman who showed him so much compassion and strength.

"What if I run into someone I know?"

"You'll know what to say."

"Like I'm dying of pneumonia. Like all those fake
obituaries," he said, kicking the coffee table. "Fucking
closet cases. Even in death." Jasmine felt the weepies
coming on. James scolded, *Be a man. Only sissies cry.*

But Jasmine was female, too. "In my obit, I want you to put that I died of AIDS. I want everyone to know."

He held onto the seat of the wheelchair and winced as he pulled himself up. The smell of barbecue wafting in from the open door reminded him of summers back in Kansas City, his mom cooking the catfish that he and his dad caught in the Missouri River, his dog Corky—was she still alive?—joyful memories that always left a wake of loneliness.

Today was supposed to be happy, floats with dancing bare-chested boys, banners, dykes on bikes.

Donna shoved the wheelchair forward. "I've brought water and trail mix."

"Poor substitute for poppers and quaaludes."

Donna laughed, pushed him outside, and shut the door.

The ocean air breathed vitality into his frail body. He raised his face to the sun and began to gather life like flowers. A bouquet of drifting purple and orange balloons floated high toward the swirling white splashes in a blue background. He heard applause and whistles as he watched a float pass by on Park Boulevard. "Go faster, Donna. I don't want to miss anything." For just one afternoon he wanted to wave the rainbow flag and cheer the parade on and forget about himself and all the dying young men.

1992

L.A. Riots

A black cloud of smoke near the intersection of Florence and Normandie drifted toward Mrs. Kim's California Dry Cleaning store in South Central Los Angeles. She turned the sign to closed and locked the door. Her husband phoned telling her to come home. The jury had acquitted the four white police officers accused of beating Rodney King. Trouble had begun.

She'd seen the video of the policemen clubbing the man when he was down. Didn't seem right.

The Kims, in their 50s, socialized with and hired only other Koreans. With their two daughters, they lived the American Dream in a Korean cocoon.

A year before, Soon Ja Du shot Latasha Harlins, a black teenager, in the back of the head in Du's convenience store and spent no time in jail. Since then, Mrs. Kim's black customers would grab their clothes and leave without saying good-bye. She didn't kill the girl, but she felt guilty.

Mrs. Kim hurried as she took the money out of the cash register and put it in a bag with the day's receipts. She wanted to leave before Mrs. Johnson came for her 6:00 Wednesday pick-up. She was a good customer, and they used to make friendly chitchat about their children. But an awkwardness had grown between her and the tall black woman with dark-red hair and pretty fingernails.

Mrs. Kim grabbed her keys. She remembered the folding security gate had to be closed, but when she got to the door, she saw Mrs. Johnson park her car. Mrs. Kim rushed to the back and hid, waiting for the woman to leave.

• • •

No justice, that's what Mrs. Johnson thought when she parked her car in front of the dry cleaning store. Times like this made her heart drag, made her so angry she wanted to go to that Simi Valley Courthouse and burn it down, down to where her heart lay. Then she saw the closed sign on the door and caught the birdlike figure of Mrs. Kim scurrying away.

Ever since the Du woman went free, Mrs. Kim, once good-hearted and sociable, never looked her in the eye, never smiled, not even a good-bye.

She considered changing cleaners but she'd been going to the Kims for years. She liked how they cleaned her hospital uniforms and choir robe, and could depend on her weekly 6:00 pick-up.

KFWB reported incidents of rioting. Mrs. Johnson locked her car. Smoke funnels dotted the late April sky. She wanted to get her cleaning and get home to her husband and two sons.

As she walked to the door, she didn't like the unchristian feeling she had toward Koreans she did business with, but why treat all black people as if we were going to rob them?

Mrs. Johnson knocked on the door. With no answer, she pounded. "I saw you, Mrs. Kim," she shouted, rattling the door. "I need my clothes *now!*"

• • •

Embarrassed, Mrs. Kim came out from the back. Trembling, she unlocked the door and opened it. "So sorry. Husband wants me home."

She went behind the counter and reached for the conveyor switch when a loud crash spun her around.

Mrs. Johnson shrieked.

Normandie
7200 S
Av
Florence

Across the street, young men were throwing bricks at Mr. Choi's liquor store. They ransacked his business, darting out with cases of beer and cartons of cigarettes.

"Call the police," Mrs. Johnson shouted.

"Line dead."

A mob of looters smashed the windows of Mr. Lee's shoe repair shop. Rioters charged down the block, raiding stores then setting them on fire.

Security alarms blared over car horns, breaking glass, screams, and hooting.

Mrs. Kim sobbed. She watched, paralyzed by the violence as real as the Korean War of her childhood. The whole block went up in flames. "Oh no, they come for me."

Mrs. Johnson shouted, "Do you have a gun?"

Mrs. Kim turned to answer when a brick crashed through her front window. Glass shattered. They both screamed.

"No. Ball bat. We go out back."

Mrs. Johnson ran around the counter and snatched the bat from Mrs. Kim.

• • •

A loud boom rocked the building. Mrs. Johnson ran to the window. In the alley, a gang of teenagers was smashing car windows, pouring gasoline inside, and torching them.

One of the boys wore a Lakers jersey, another an LA Dodger cap turned backwards. Those boys could be her sons. Their rage was her rage.

Yet she held onto Dr. King's teachings of love and nonviolence.

"We trapped," Mrs. Kim cried, standing beside her. "Where police?"

The front of the shop exploded. The smell of burning plastic overwhelmed them.

Mrs. Johnson slid the bolt back and opened the door.

"I go too."

"No. Stay here."

Ball bat in hand, Mrs. Johnson, as pissed-off as she'd ever been, walked into the alley, into the smell of gasoline swirling in thick smoke and the sound of sirens wailing and dogs howling. Her heart ached for her people, but burning down their own neighborhood? She prayed to Jesus as she walked into the madness.

"You with the Laker jersey," she yelled. "I know your mama." She choked the handle of the club. "You think she'd be proud of you?"

"You wigg'n out, lady," he said, strutting toward her, moving his hands gangsta style. "You don't know nothin."

At 5'10" she was at least 4 inches taller. She took a step forward. "Get your homies and get out of here, or I'll tell your mama what you've been up to."

They were locked in a stare down.

His dawgs stopped to watch.

"C'mon," Laker jersey said to his homeboys. "You don't tell my mama nothin," he muttered and swaggered away.

Mrs. Kim ran to her van, unlocked it, started the engine, and opened the passenger door.

Mrs. Johnson jumped in. She thanked the Lord for their deliverance.

"Glad you come," Mrs. Kim said with tears in her eyes as she floored the gas peddle and tore down the alley.

STEPPING
UP
A Short Story Collection
DC
DIAMONDOPOLOUS

Acclaim for *Stepping Up*

(A Short Story Collection)

This incandescent collection of stories by writer DC Diamondopolous knocked me to the ground. Heartbreaking, revealing, numbing, and provocative, each page touched me, not lightly, but with a fist of shards.
> ~ **Sharon Lovejoy,** author of *Running Out of Night*

This collection is a vigorous examination of American culture—a gutsy probe into social divide, including fractious family dynamics. Diamondopolous writes with exuberance and emotional understanding. It's the human element that reaches out and pulls us in.
> ~ **Sherry Shahan,** *Purple Daze: A Far Out Trip,* 1965

Each story in this collection is a passport to places where characters are challenged to be their true selves, no matter the risk. Every protagonist compels the reader to revisit them. Their diverse stories span eras and genres, yet always target the heart. DC Diamondopolous creates worlds with striking images and surprising twists that resonate long after the last line. Stepping Up is an astonishing tour de force.
> ~ **Cindy Rankin,** author of *Under the Ashes*

About the Author

DC Diamondopolous is a multi award-winning short story and flash fiction writer with hundreds of stories published internationally in print and online magazines, literary journals, and anthologies. DC's stories have appeared in: *Penmen Review, Progenitor, 34th Parallel, So It Goes: The Literary Journal of the Kurt Vonnegut Museum and Library, Lunch Ticket,* and others. Nominated twice in 2020 for the Pushcart Prize and in 2017 and 2020 for Best of the Net Anthology, DC was also a Finalist in 2019, 2020, and 2021 in ScreenCrafts Cinematic Short Story Contest. In addition to other awards, she has been recognized with two Honorable Mentions from the Soul-Making Keats Literary Competition. Her collection of short stories, *Stepping Up,* was published by *Impspired* in 2020. Coming from a theatrical background, DC began writing while touring with an improvisation company. She lives on the California central coast with her wife and animals.

DCDiamondopolous.com